Cy Warman, Fitz Mac

The Silver Queen

A Romance of the Early Days of Creed Camp

Cy Warman, Fitz Mac

The Silver Queen
A Romance of the Early Days of Creed Camp

ISBN/EAN: 9783744772877

Printed in Europe, USA, Canada, Australia, Japan

Cover: Foto ©Andreas Hilbeck / pixelio.de

More available books at **www.hansebooks.com**

THE
SILVER QUEEN

A ROMANCE OF THE

EARLY DAYS OF CREEDE CAMP

BY

CY WARMAN AND FITZ MAC

ILLUSTRATIONS BY ZELLA NEILL.

DENVER
THE GREAT DIVIDE PUBLISHING COMPANY
1894

THE SILVER QUEEN.

I.

DENVER, March 15, 1892.

MY DEAR MR. WARMAN :—I notice
by the papers that you are getting
ready to start a daily in Creede. Your
courage is worthy of all astonishment.
Don't you know the gamblers there
will shoot you full of holes, and perhaps spoil the only suit you've got fit
to be buried in, before your paper
reaches the tenth number ? Whatever
you do, wear your old clothes and keep
your Sunday suit nice for emergencies.
The boys will all chip in and give you
a big funeral, but we haven't any of us
got a spare coat fit to bury you in ; so
take care of your Prince Albert and
wear your corduroys till the question is
settled one way or the other, for if

anything should happen, it would mor-
tify the boys to have to bury in his
shirt-sleeves the only poet Colorado has
produced.

Well, you are in for it, I suppose,
and nothing will stop you, and being
in, there is nothing for it now but to
" bear thyself so thine enemy may be-
ware thee," or in other words, heel

yourself and face the music like a man.
Whatever else you do, don't show the
white feather, for the honor of the
press is in your keeping, and if you
will immolate yourself, we expect you
to die game and not with a bullet in
your back. Don't worry one minute
about the obituary notices. That will
be all right. The
boys will all see
you through in
good shape and
the papers here
will all turn rules
and celebrate
your virtues in
such halting me-
ter as can be
mustered.

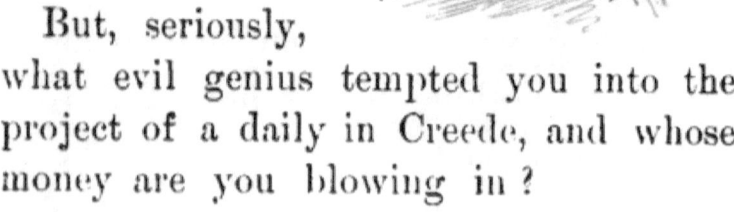

But, seriously,
what evil genius tempted you into the
project of a daily in Creede, and whose
money are you blowing in?

If your ambition is to establish a reputation for courage—going into such a lair of hobos, gamblers and all-round toughs—most people will think it absurdly superfluous in a man—a western man at least—who makes no concealment of the fact, in this *fin de siecle* era, that he perpetrates poetry and is willing to make his living by it—if he can.

I have no wish to discourage you, Cy, in your present heroic enterprise; but I think, myself, it is wholly unnecessary as an evidence of pluck, after all the poetry you have perpetrated. Everybody knows that a poet—a western poet, especially—takes his life in his hands whenever he approaches a publisher, as recklessly as the man who runs sheep onto a cow range. Of course, no western man would feel any compunction in killing a

poet, considering that whatever atten-
tion they command in the East makes
against our reputation out here for
practical horse-sense and energy, and
tends to make the underwriters and
money-lenders suspicious and raise the
rates of interest and insurance.

I would n't hurt your feelings for the
world, for I confess I like your poetry
myself, but I think you owe the singular immunity you have enjoyed in
Denver above other poets who have
bit the dust or emigrated eastward, to
the openly-expressed admiration and
affection of Myron Reed and Jim Belford and a few other reckless cranks
who have intrenched themselves against
"the practical horse-sense" which is
the pride of our people. As, instance:
I happened into that gun-store in the
Tabor Block yesterday to provide myself with a jointed fishing-rod against

what time I should come down to
your funeral—for they tell me the Upper Rio Grande swarms with trout, and
I thought I might like to cast a fly,
even so early, after see-
ing you planted, and be-
ing shown the spot where
you fell. For I fancy
some of those toughs
whose hearts your in-
spired verses had touched,
commiserating my tears,

would come to me and take me gently
by the hand and lead me down to the coroner's office to show me the hole in the
breast of your coat—for I never have done
you the wrong to imagine the hole anywhere *but* in the breast where the re-
morseless bullet tore its way to your
brave heart. And then the tender-
hearted tough, wiping his eyes with his
sleeve, should draw me away and lead

me up the street "to see where it happened," and that he should halt at a certain spot in front of a great flourishing saloon and gambling hall, where I should catch a glimpse through the windows, of battered and frowzy girls in dirty, trailing calico "tea-gowns" and thin slippers, drinking at the bar with the cheaper class of the gamblers or with befuddled miners they were preparing to rob, and he should say: "'Twas right here—right where I'm standin'—and poor Cy, he wuz goin' along and he wuz n't sayin' nothin' to nobody, 'n' I was standin' right across the street there, in the door of Minnie Monroe's place, an' Min she wuz leanin' over my shoulder and we wuz both lookin' right across at the saloon where Soapy Smith wuz standin' in the door, readin' a newspaper out loud to Bob Ford an' a lot o' them low-down girls that hangs around there after breakfast till they strike a treat; an' at every word Soapy he was rippin' out oaths an' shakin' his fist, an' Min. she says to me: 'Bill, there's a row on, les' go over and see what's up.' 'N' jest at that minute along comes poor Cy— mindin' his own business 'n' sayin' nothin' to nobody—an' that's what I'll swear to 'fore the grand jury, mister, if I'm called, an' Min, she'll swear to the same thing. Nothin' would n't a' happened, fur everybody's back wuz turned, only fur one o' them lowdown trollops stuck her head out o' the door and s'ys, 'There's the —— —— ——, now,' and Bob Ford he looked over his shoulder 'n' s'ys, 'Sure 'nough Soapy, there goes your man.'

"Min an' me heard every word jest

as plain as a pin. Cy heard it, too, and
he knowed what it meant. He wuz
game—I'll say that fur him—'n' faced
about 'n' reached fur his gun quicker
'n' the jerk of a lamb's tail in fly
time, but Soapy got there first, 'cause
he'd rushed out with his gun cocked,
and it wuz all day with poor Cy 'fore
you could say Jack Robinson."

"Reached for his gun?" (in imagi-
nation I inquire doubtingly)—"then he
was—"

"Oh, yes, he was heeled. Cy wuz n't
no chump. He knowed he was takin'
his life in his hands when he jumped
that gang an' began to roast them in
his paper. He knowed they'd lay fur
him an' do him up if they ever got
the drop on him 'fore he could draw.
But oh, say, if poor Cy had just had
a show—or even *half* a show—would n't
he shot the everlastin' stuffin' out o'

that crowd quicker 'n' a cat could lick her ear! That's what he would, mister, fur he was game an' he could handle a gun beautiful. But" (in my fancy your worthy tough always draws his sleeve across his face at this juncture) "I suppose it *had* to be— prob'ly it was God'l Mighty's will. There's the pole over yander front o' Min's place we strung Soapy and Bob to, an' there wuz n't no inquest on *them* — not much there wuz n't, for the coroner himself helped at the lynchin' —*everybody* helped 'ceptin' that pigeon-livered cad of a preacher. He wanted to deliver a lecture to the crowd on the majesty of the law an' that kind o' thing, but he got left on his little game that time. Oh, he's too slow for *this* camp, mister. The preacher that can't keep up with the band wagon, ain't got no business monkeyin' around a live mining camp like Creede."

But bless my stars, how my anxiety for you has drawn me into digression? I started to tell you what happened at the gun-store. You know it's a place where some clever men drop in and lounge a bit and swap sporting stories and smoke a friendly cigar. I heard some one call me to the rear, and going back, I found Belford and their reverences, Tom Uzzell and My- ron Reed—God bless their manly souls—and one or two others I did not know. And your friend, the Reverend Myron, was reading aloud to the crowd that fanciful little jingle you had in yes- terday's *Times* about the beautiful but

willful maid who wandered down to
the shore of sin and got snatched
back by some compunctious Joseph before the undertow caught her, or language to that general effect ;—forgive
me, I have n't been able to read it
myself and cannot recall a line of it
although I recognized it as a gem.

Well, you could see the little crowd
was being affected, for Mr. Reed was
delivering it with exquisite feeling,
and when he had finished, there was
a general glance of admiration all
round ; and Mr. Uzzell remarked that
there was a fine sermon—I think, on
reflection, that he said a fine, *strong*
sermon—in the verses ; and your
friend Reed smiled. Then Belford,
in a characteristic burst of rhetoric,
declared that " The Muses must have
kissed in his cradle, the fellow
who wrote those lines." And your

friend, the Reverend Myron, smiled out loud, and Belford glanced around the crowd for approval.

I should n't consider that fraternal magnanimity required me to repeat these flattering expressions to you, Cy, only that I feel your doom draws nigh. It is borne in upon me with all the psychic force of a prophecy that you are fated to perish by the ignominious hand of our own and only Soapy, if you persist in starting that daily. You can't run a daily without saying something, and you can't say anything that ought to be said without giving mortal offense to the toughs who are running that camp, and you can't give offense to them without getting shot. It is an ancient saying that "a word to the wise is sufficient"; but it were better to say, as experience proves, that a word to the wise is generally superfluous. Be wise, Cyrus, in your day and generation. Seek fame in other fields. Open a boarding-house or an undertaker's shop, or both. This will give you a chance to study human nature in all its phases. It is the school for a poet and philosopher. Don't miss the opportunity. Don't waste your promising young life writing poetry or running a daily paper to reform the morals of a mining camp. Either is sure to bring you to an ignominious grave. But if, in spite of my prayers and tears, you will persist, send me your paper. I shall have a curiosity to see what sort of a stagger you make at moulding the protoplasm of public opinion into a cellular structure of moral impulse. Send me the paper, *sure.* So-long. God protect you.

Always,

Fitz-Mac.

P. S.—Now, may confusion take my muddled brains, but I have overlooked the very thing I started to write you about.

The inclosed letter of introduction will make you acquainted with Miss Polly Parsons, a young girl whom I have known from childhood, and in whose welfare I take a serious interest. She is a bright and beautiful girl—and a thoroughly good girl, let me remark—and I want her to know you and feel that she has a friend in you on whom she can call for counsel and protection if need be.

She is under the necessity, not only of making her own living, but of contributing to the support of her father's family. Her mother and little brother are here, living in two rooms, but her father is in Chicago. I knew the family there years ago when they were very rich, and surrounded by every luxury—fine home on Michigan avenue, carriages and footman and all that. But Parsons went broke a few years ago on grain speculations, and the worst of it is, he lost his courage with his money and is now a broken-spirited man, doing the leg work for brokers and leaving his family to shift for themselves, or pretty nearly so. I suppose it is really impossible for the poor fellow to help them very much or he would, for he loved his wife and children. Polly had every advantage

that money could purchase till the old man
failed, and she is finely educated. She is a girl
of great courage and has an ambition to make
a business woman of herself and help her father
onto his feet again.   She has some of his
genius for   bold, speculative action, and   has
taken up stenography and typewriting—not as
an end but only as a means.

I am very much afraid she has made a serious   misstep in going to Creede and that she
will get herself hopelessly compromised before
she is done with it.

She has gone down with that Sure Thing
Mining Company outfit and I suspect they are
a bad lot; but some of them knew her father
in the past, and thus gained her confidence.
She is too pretty a girl and too inexperienced
to be exposed to the associations of a mining
camp like Creede, where there are so few decent
women, without great danger. She has got courage and an earnest purpose, and those qualities
are a woman's best safeguard; but still, she is
only a girl of nineteen or twenty and she does n't
realize what a delicate thing a woman's reputation is. It was sheer recklessness for her to go
down there; but I did n't know it till after she
was off.   Her mother got anxious after she had
let her go and came to see me about it.   I believe—without   positively   knowing—that   the

outfit she has gone to are right-down scamps.
They seem to have plenty of money and they
have opened a grand office here, but they strike
me as bad eggs. A very suspicious circumstance
in regard to their motives toward her—to my
mind at least—is that they have promised her
a salary of two hundred and fifty dollars a
month. That is
simply prepos-
terous. (You
know that they
can get an army
of competent ste-
nographers and
typewriters at
one hundred dol-
lars a month, or
even less.) I don't
like the looks of

it a bit. I suspect they—or one of them—have
designs against the girl.

She is honest to the core, and they will never
accomplish her ruin—if that is what they mean.
But of course, you must understand, I am only
voicing a suspicion, and a very uncharitable one
at that; but the odor of the outfit is bad, and
they may compromise her hopelessly before she
gets her eyes open, and spoil her life.

I want you to hunt her up and keep an eye on

her, and put yourself on a square footing with
her, so that she will have confidence in you.
Above all things, see that she has a boarding
place where there is some respectable married
woman, and give her a talking to about the
camp that will open her eyes. She will take
care of herself all right if she is once put on
her guard.

I want you to understand she is no pick-up
for any rake to trifle with; but a woman is a
woman—you know that, Cy, as well as I do—
and youth is youth.

She is a good telegrapher—unusually good, I
imagine. I mention this so that you may get
her employment if that job she has gone to
looks at all scaly, and likely to compromise her.

She has great force of character—her father's
temperament before he broke down—and she has
taken up all these things to fit herself for that
business career to which she aspires. Don't be
deceived by her suave and amiable manner into
thinking her a weakling, for she has got *immense*
force of character, and she perfectly believes she
is going to have a business career.

I have told her in the letter that you are
engaged to the nicest girl in Denver, so as to
put you on a confidential footing, and head off
your falling in love with her yourself. Be a
brother to her, Cy, and keep her out of trouble.

God knows you are wicked enough yourself to scent wickedness from afar and see any danger in the path of an attractive girl without experience. Look her up at once—*at once*, mind you —and let me have a good account of yourself as soon as possible.   Affectionately,

FITZ-MAC.

II.

CREEDE, Colo., March 17, 1892.
To FITZ-MAC, Denver, Colo.

My Dear Fitz :—Your letter came here yesterday along with the circulars sent by those peddlers of printing presses and printer's ink, but I have been so busy getting things in shape to start the *Chronicle*, that there has been little time to look after the beautiful creature of whom you write. Thousands of stenographers have gone from home to take positions where the pay was better, and no great harm has resulted, and why you have become so thoroughly alarmed over the young lady,

I am unable to understand. If, as your letter would indicate, she has lived all her life in Chicago, she is perfectly safe in Creede.

I went to the station, or rather to the place where the train stops, this morning, but saw no one who would answer the description of your young lady. Of the three hundred passengers, not more than ten were women, and very ordinary looking women at that.

I know that I could find your friend if she is in the camp, by turning your letter over to Hartigan, the city editor, but he is a handsome young Irishman who quotes poetry by the mile, and the fact that he has a wife in Denver would not prevent him from opening a flirtation at the first meeting.

No, she is better off with the smooth young man than with Hartigan. Tabor,

who is to be the local man, is single,
but little better than the city editor.
He is very susceptible and would
fall in love with the young woman
and, of course, neglect his work. A
morning paper whose editor is threat-
ened with matrimony should keep its
working force out of the breakers.

The worst feature, so far as I can
see, is the fact that I am unable to locate the Sure Thing Mining Company;
but I hope when Mr. Wygant, the advertising man, comes in, he may be
able to enlighten me on this point. It
is my purpose, so far as possible, to
carry advertisements in the *Chronicle*
for none but good companies; and to
guard against any impositions, I employed a man who is well known and
well acquainted with all the fake
schemes; and further, that he may have
no serious temptations, he will be

paid a salary instead of a commission.

However, there may be a Sure Thing Mining Company, and it may be all right; but I have failed so far to learn anything about it. The camp continues to boom. One of the fraternity shot a thumb off the hand of a fellow sport at Bannigan's last night. I have not taken in the town yet, although the temptation has been very great. Both the rival theaters have tendered me a box, and assured me that I would not be "worked."

Until now, I never knew what an important personage the editor of a morning paper was. The city marshal called at the office yes-  terday with a half dozen bottles of beer, which he gave to Freckled Jimmie, the devil, with

the explanation that he understood that
the editor was a Democrat.

I have made a good impression on
society here, I think. The first man I
was introduced to when I stepped from
the train, was Bob Ford, who, in connection with the Governor of Missouri,
removed Jesse James some ten years
ago. (He is a pale, sallow fellow with
a haunted look, and he is always
nervous when his back is to the door.)
Fitz, there is a great deal of wickedness in this world, and in a mining
camp they make no attempt at hiding
it.

If I were not very busy, I should
be very unhappy here. From morning
till night and from night until morning, the ceaseless tramp, tramp, on
wooden walks of the comers and goers
is painfully monotonous. Once in a
while a pistol-shot echoes in the cañon,

and the saddest thing is that it is so common that the players scarcely turn from the tables to see who has fallen in the fight.

And men move on, and give no heed
To life or death,—and this is Creede.

By-and-by it will be different. When we have a city government, crime will be punished. The gambling and other disreputable resorts will be confined to their own quarter, and Creede will become the greatest silver camp on earth.

After paying one thousand dollars on our building and as much on our press and outfit, we had one thousand two hundred and fifty dollars to our credit.

This morning's mail brought a letter from Mr. Sanders inclosing a Last Chance check for five hundred dollars. The same mail brought D. H.

M.'s check for two hundred and fifty dollars with the request that I accept it with his compliments, but he would have no stock. Now these people are all Republicans, and they know that I will run a Democratic paper. In the language of the songster, "That is love."

I want to say that you do my friend Smith a great injustice, when, in your day-dream, you make him my slayer. He is my personal body-guard. He is also a bitter enemy of Ford's. Mark you, these men will meet some day— I say some *day*, for it's never night in Creede,—and whether he do kill Sapolio or Sapolio do kill him, or both,—especially the latter,—the incident will render my position all the more secure.

When Governor Routt was here working the shells on the Smart

Alecks who came to camp to buy corner lots cheap, I bought a lot on the shores of the West Willow. The selvage of my property was swept by the rushing waters of the busy little brook; and I gave it out that I wanted that particular lot to have water-power for my press. Of course, all were anxious to aid in the establishment of a morning paper, and the lot came to me at three hundred dollars, the minimum price, which is just thirty times its value. The lot next to mine was reserved by the State for the use of the little brook.

A speculative pirate, by the name of Streepy, built a house over the river and turned the stream through my lot, so now all I own is the river.

In closing, let me assure you that I will do all in my power to locate the young woman, and advise you.

Yours truly,

Cy Warman.

III.

Denver, March 20, 1892.

My Dear Warman :—Yours of the 17th, after some unaccounted-for delay, has but just reached me. Perhaps your gifted postmistress had not time to read it  at once, and so held it over till leisure should serve her curiosity ; or she may have found unexpected difficulty in deciphering your ingeniously atrocious writing, which I can imagine would only increase the curiosity of a gifted woman.

I once lived where the postmaster, a man of intellectual inclinations, was

very slow at reading manuscript, being
obliged to spell out the words labori-
ously, and I found the delay occasioned
by the interest he took in studying my
epistolary style, to improve his mind, a
great annoyance. But a bright thought
struck me one day, and I employed a
typewriter. After that there was but
little delay, for he could read print
very well. I offer you the value of this
experience, not at all on my account,
for I can generally manage to make
out what you are writing about pretty
closely, but to promote expedition in
mail service. It occurs to me to mention, however, *en passant*, that if you
fail in that newspaper enterprise, you
still have a bright career for your pen
before you in the Orient, marking tea-
chests. Do not imagine that I am
complaining when I say that your
friends would find more time to love

you if you would employ a typewriter.

But all this is neither here nor there. I am in despair at the devil-may-care tone in which you write about Miss Parsons, and I am really alarmed about her not having arrived. She certainly could not have had much money by her to make a leisurely trip of it, stopping off to see the towns and the scenery *en route*.

Her mother was in a few moments ago, and not having heard from her, is naturally anxious, but I affected to consider it nothing. As a matter of fact, I regard it as very strange and alarming, considering that she left Denver with a man I strongly suspect is a scamp, and if the Sure Thing Mining Company has no office there, the worst is to be feared. It looks very bad.

My hope is, that in your indifference to my request, not appreciating the seriousness of the case, you have not looked around. I suppose it is a matter of no little trouble to find any one, unless you happen upon him, in such a mad rush as ·has set in for Creede. I met Whitehead of the *News*,

who is just back from there, and he says that not only are the platforms even of the cars crowded, but men actually ride on top from Alamosa over, in the craze to get there. What insanity! How can such a rush of people be housed and fed in a camp that contained but five little cabins ninety days ago! But it is all grist for your mill, of course.

Now, *can* I make you understand the seriousness of this case? You cer-

tainly know how easy it is for a vil-
lain to compromise a young and pretty
girl like Miss Parsons in a place like
Creede, and you know that a young
girl compromised is already half ruined.
As I have said, Polly is a pure-minded,
honest girl of great force of character.
I consider her taking up and mastering
shorthand and typewriting and tele-
graphing, sufficient evidence of that;
but she is inexperienced and unsuspi-
cious, and may find herself undone before she realizes her danger. Besides,
that fellow Ketchum is a handsome,
unscrupulous man, with an oily tongue
in his head.

I have to go to Chicago to-night and
I shall be absent two or three weeks,
otherwise I would run down to Creede
myself—so great is my anxiety about
this girl, whom I have known from
her cradle.

I must leave the matter in your hands—if I can only make you look at it seriously. Her mother's address is No. 1796 California street—Mrs. Matilda Parsons. Communicate with her if necessary. I have told her about writing to you, etc.

Probably, while in Chicago, I shall be able to look up her father and will talk with him about the matter. Now please take up this matter seriously and oblige me forever.

Au revoir, and good luck to you with the paper.

FITZ-MAC.

IV.

CREEDE, COLO., March 25, '92.

MY DEAR FITZ:—Since receiving your second letter, I have left nothing undone in the way of keeping a constant lookout for Miss Parsons, for I

see how terribly in earnest you are.
Yesterday I took dinner at a little restaurant in Upper Creede, and when the
girl came to take my order she almost
took my breath. There was something
about her that
told me that she
was new at the
business; and I
began to be
hopeful that she
might be the
young lady for
whom I had been looking for
the past week. When the
rest had left the table, I asked
for a second cup of coffee,
and when she brought it, I made an attempt to engage the girl in conversa-
tion.

"You are very busy here," I said.

"Yes," she answered, with a slight

raise of the eyebrows, and just a hint of a smile playing round her mouth.

"I presume you get very tired by closing time," I ventured.

"We never close," she said ; and again I noticed the same movement of the eyes.

I knew she thought I was endeavoring to build up an acquaintance, and it annoyed me. If there is one thing I dislike, it is to be taken for a masher when I am not trying to mash.

"Have n't I seen you in Denver ?"

"Perhaps."

"Have n't I seen you with Mr. Ketchum ?"

"Perhaps."

"Do you know Mr. Ketchum ?" I asked with some embarrassment.

"Do you ?"

"Well, not very intimately," was my

somewhat uncertain reply. " Is he in town ? "

The girl laughed in real earnest. When she did compose herself, she asked, " Are you a reporter for the new paper ? "

I told her I was not, and then I asked her if she could tell me where Mr. Ketchum's office was.

It was down the street near the Holy Moses saloon, she said ; and I congratulated myself upon having gotten a straight and lucid reply from her.

" Is he in town ? " was my next question.

" He was at this table when you came in. Don't you know him ? "

" Not very well," said I.

" Then how do you know you saw me with Mr. Ketchum ? "

I said he must have changed.

" No," said the girl, showing some

spunk. "You don't know him. You never saw him; but you are trying to be funny. Your name is Lon Harti-gan, and I am dead onto you."

"O, break!—break away!" said a chemical blonde, as she swept in from the kitchen, coming to the res-cue. of her "partner," as she called her. "The girls from the Beebee put us onto you and that fel-low from New York. You can't come none of your monkey doodle bus-iness here. Mr. Ketchum is the nicest man 'at eats here and he always leaves a dollar under his plate." And the drug-store blonde snapped her fingers under my nose, whirled on her heel, and banging a soiled towel into a barrel that stood by the door leading to the kitchen, she swept from the room.

"Will you bring me some hot coffee?" I said, softly, to the girl with her own hair.

"You misjudge me," I began, as she set it down.

"I am sorry," she replied with a hemi-smile that hinted of sympathy, but is worse than no sympathy.

"Now, see here," I began, "I'll tell you my name if you'll tell me yours. My name is Warman."

"My name is Boyd—Inez Boyd," said the girl, "and I am sorry to have talked as I have, to you."

"Don't mention it," said I, as I left the room.

Outside I saw a sign which read: "The Sure Thing Mining and Milling Company, Capital Stock, $1,000,000."

The next moment I stood in the outer office, saw a sign on a closed door: "F. I. Ketchum—Private."

I opened a little wooden gate, stepped
to the private entrance and knocked.
A tall, good-looking man of thirty-five
to forty, with soft gray
hair, came out and closed
the door quickly.

"Is this Mr. Ketchum?"
I asked.

"Yes sir, what can I
do for you?"

Now that was a sticker.
It had not occurred to
me that to call a man
out of his private office
one ought to have some business.

"I'm the editor of the *Chronicle* and
I just dropped in to get acquainted. I
have heard of your company."

The man looked black. "We are
not looking for newspaper notoriety,"
he said, without offering me a seat. In
short, he did n't rave over me, as some

of the real estate men did, and after asking how the property of the company was looking, I went away. Poor as I am, I would have given twenty to have seen into the "Private" room.

I write all this in detail, that you may know how hard I have tried to do my duty to you as a friend, and to the poor unfortunate girl, as a man. I shall have more time from now on, as I have for my superintendent and general master mechanic, Mr. J. D. Vaughan, who can make a newspaper, from the writing of the editorial page, to the mailing list. In the past, as now, he has always been with distinguished men. He was with Artemus Ward at Cleveland, Wallace Gruelle, at Louisville, Bartley Campbell, at New Orleans, Will L. Visscher when he ran the "Headlight," on board the steamer Richmond running between Louisville

and New Orleans, and with Field and
Rothaker on the Denver *Tribune*.

We got out our first issue Monday,
and I feel a great deal better. It has
been the dream of my life to have a
daily paper, and we have got one now
that is all wool and as
wide as the press will
print. I have this line under the heading :

"Politics: Free Coinage ;
Religion : Creede."

I think that line will last.
It is what we must live for
and hope for. Of course, we
expect to lose money for a few months ;
but if the camp continues to grow, the
Chronicle Publishing Company will be
a good venture. There are many hard-
ships to be endured in a mining-camp.
The printers had to stand in an un-
covered house and set type while the

snow drifted around their collars. They held a meeting in the rear office Sunday, organized a printers' union, fixed a schedule to suit themselves—fifty cents a thousand ; and, in order that I might not feel lonely, I was made an honorary member of the union.

Mr. George W. Childs was taken in at the same time. My salary is to be fifty dollars a week ; but I don't intend to draw my salary until the paper is on a paying basis.

We have not got our motor in place yet, and I had to pay two Mexicans twelve dollars for turning the press the first night. Coal is ten dollars a ton ; coal oil sixty cents a gallon. We use a ton of coal every twenty-four hours and five gallons of oil every night. It was a novel sight to see the newsboys running here and there through the willows, climbing up the steep sides of the gulch to the tents and cabins crying "Morning *Chronicle!*" where the mountain lion and the grizzly bear had their homes but six months ago. The interesting feature in the first issue is a three - column account of Gambler Joe Simmons' funeral. It tells how the gang stood at the grave and drank "To Joe's soul over there —if there is any over there."

Yours always,

Cy WARMAN.

IV.

CREEDE, COLO., March 28, 1892.

DEAR FITZ :—Three days ago I wrote you that I had located Mr. Ketchum but failed to find the girl. Yesterday being Sunday, I went down to the hot springs at Wagon Wheel

Gap to spend the day. At the hotel I met Mrs. McCleland, of Alamosa, and while we were conversing, a lady commenced to sing in the parlor. The soft notes that came from the piano mingled with a voice so full of soulful melody, that I stopped talking and listened. "Do you like music?" asked the good lady from the San Luis. "There is but one thing sweeter," I said, "and that is poetry —the music of the soul. Take me in, won't you?"

We entered so softly that the young woman at the piano failed to notice our coming, and sang on to the end of the piece.

"La Paloma!" How different from the strains I had heard during the past

week, from the Umpah band in front
of the Olympic Theater.

When she had finished, the singer
turned, blushed, and rising, advanced
toward my friend, holding out her
hand ; and I was surprised and pleased
to hear Mrs. Mc. say :
"Well, I want to know
—are you here ?"

The young lady ac-
knowledged that she was,
and went into a long ex-
planation that she had
concluded to stop at the
springs until matters were in a little
better shape at Creede.

"Where is Mr. ——, Mr. ——," stam-
mered Mrs. Mc.

"Oh, he's in Creede," said the young
lady, as she shot a glance at me which
was followed by a becoming blush.
"He is so busy at the mines ; they

work a great many men, you know."

All this time I had been looking over Mrs. McCleland's shoulder into an exceedingly bright and interesting face.

"Oh, I beg your pardon," said **the** good lady, "this is Mr. Warman, Miss Parsons."

I don't know for the life of me, whether I s a i d "H o w d·y," or "Good-by," I was dazed. I had forgotten the while I looked into that beautiful face, that such a person lived as Polly Parsons, and when it came to me all at once like the firing of a blast, it took the wind out of my sails and left me helpless in mid-ocean.

"Where did you meet Miss Parsons?" I asked, when the young lady had left the room.

"At Alamosa, some two weeks ago, she stopped at our hotel, and I did n't like the looks of the man she was with; so I asked her to sleep in a spare room just off from my own.

"I heard him trying to persuade her to go to Creede with him the next day, but could not understand what her argument was, except that she would not go to Creede until there was something for her to do."

"Who was this man?" I asked.

"His name is Ketchum; he is connected with the Sure Thing Mining Company."

"At last!" I said with a sigh that was really a relief to me.

After luncheon, I gave the letter you sent, to Miss Parsons, and I watched her face while she read it.

Of one of two things I am con-
vinced ; either she loves you and was
glad to see that letter, or she hates
you and will do as much
for me. That is as near
as you can guess a pretty
woman.

"If there's anything I
can do for you, Miss
Parsons —" "O, I am
quite capable of getting
along alone," she said.
"I thank you, of course,
but there is nothing ; I
am promised a good position in Mr.
Ketchum's office as soon as they get
things in shape. I have some ready
money with me, enough to pay my
expenses at the hotel."

"You will not find so pleasant a
hotel in Creede as this, Miss Parsons.
The Pattons are nice people, and it

would be better, I think, for you to remain here until a position is open for you," I ventured by way of advice.

"Mr. Ketchum has engaged a room for me over the Albany Restaurant," she said, "and he is to call here for me to-morrow."

"But, Miss Parsons," said I, "do you know what sort of a place that is?"

"I know, sir, that Mr. Ketchum would not take me to an improper place," and she gave her head a twist that told me that my advice was not wanted.

"I beg your pardon, Miss Parsons," said I, by way of explanation; "I was thinking of the Albany Theater building; the restaurant may be all right. But I was thinking only of your welfare."

"Thank you," she said, but she meant "Don't trouble yourself."

"Good-by, Miss Parsons," I said, extending my hand. "Hope I may have the pleasure of meeting you in Creede."

"I go to Creede to-morrow," she said as she gave me a warm, plump hand and said "Good-by."

Fitz, forgive me for being so slow; but you forgot to tell me how beautiful she was; the Poet of the Kansas City *Star* would say: "Her carriage, face and figure are perfection; and her smile is a shimmer-tangled day-dream, as she drifts adown the aisle." Such eyes! like miniature seas, set about with weeping willows, and hair like ripening grain, with the sunlight sifting through it.   Good-by,

Cy Warman.

V.

Grand Pacific Hotel,
            Chicago, April 8.
Dear Cy :—Your two letters of the

25th and 28th ult., forwarded from Denver, were received here only this morning on my return from Milwaukee, where I have been for the past week negotiating the sale of that Eagle Gulch mining property, in which I am interested. I think it will be a go, and if so, I shall be heeled—otherwise busted.

It was very good of you, old boy, to take so much trouble to look Miss Parsons up and to "locate" that scamp Ketchum. I shall not be anxious, now that I know you will keep an eye on her. But you are clear off, Cy, as to her loving or hating me.

No doubt she likes me a little bit, for I have long been a friend of the family; and they were always kind to me when they were rich, and I have carried pretty Polly around in my arms when she was a baby. I knew her father back in Virginia before they were married.

Pretty? I should think she is pretty. That is why I felt so particularly anxious about her going to Creede. If she had been a ewe-necked old scrub of a typewriter, with a peaked nose and a pair of gooseberry eyes in her head, do you fancy I could have been solicitous about her not being able to take care of herself or have dreamt of interesting you in her?

Cyrus, my princely buck, if there was any "peculiar light" in pretty Polly's eyes, it was admiration for your manly figure. You are too modest to ever do yourself justice.

I am glad you found Ketchum and the Sure Thing Mining Company. I had to laugh at the mystery you make of that back room into which you were not permitted to peep. No doubt he was working some pilgrim in there to whom he expected to sell stock, and did not want to be interrupted.

I met a broker the other day who knew him well here. He is a scamp, as I thought; but not exactly the kind of scamp I thought. He has had a career on the Exchange here and was once a heavy operator and made big money, but his reputation was never first-class and it has become decidedly odorous of late years through his connection with snide stock schemes of one kind and another. But he has kept out of jail and is n't a person a man can exactly refuse to speak to.

He worked a Napoleonic confidence deal in grain here, some five or six years back, and came within an ace of cleaning up a million or more on it; but the fraud was discovered and the bubble exploded, leaving him beggared both in fortune and reputation. He

had tangled a lot of respectable operators up in the scheme, so that it did
not look so very bad for him personally, and he escaped prosecution. Since
then he has figured as a promoter,
keeping himself in the shade.

Parsons, Polly's father, was the man
who discovered and defeated his fraud ;
and the story goes here, that in re-
venge, he set the trap into which Parsons fell and lost all except his honor.
Parsons has a good name here still, I
find, among the brokers, because he
made an honest settlement, although it
left him penniless and broken-spirited.
It is strange that he has n't come to see
me. I tried to find him when I first
came ; but he was always somewhere
else, and when I went to Milwakee, I
left a note for him, but have heard
nothing. I shall try to see him before I leave.

I find Ketchum has a wife and some children here, and that he does n't figure as a Lothario at all as I suspected. On the contrary, he is quite a model in his domestic relations—takes his family to church and all that, and is a shining light in the Sunday-school and the Y. M. C. A. So I fancy our pretty Polly is in no great danger from him. It is singular though, why he should have engaged the daughter of a man whom he must hate, as his confidential clerk —and at such a preposterous salary, too. It is suspicious ; but after all, it may be a freak of kindness, finding the man whose ruin he has planned so destitute. It is just as safe to take the charitable view as any, even of a scamp. Human motives are always mixed.

I cannot say when I will be at home ; but write often, directing to

Denver, and keep a brotherly eye on
our pretty Polly.   Yours,

FITZ-MAC.

VI.

GRAND PACIFIC HOTEL,
CHICAGO, April 9, 9 o'clock P. M.

DEAR WARMAN :—I must write in
great haste, for in an hour I leave for
New York. It is quite unexpected. I
expect the Milwaukee party here in a
quarter of an hour to go with me.

In all probability I shall not be
back to Denver before the first of May,
if then,—for, being in New York, I
shall probably stop and attend ' to
some other matters.

I wrote you last night, and now I
want to correct the impressions of that
letter.

When does one ever hear the last word
of a bad story. That fellow Ketchum

is even more of an all-round scoundrel
than I thought. I have heard a lot
about him to-day ; ran upon a man
who was his head book-keeper and
confidential man here in his heyday,
and whom he robbed, as he has everybody else who has had anything to do
with him. I was out looking up Parsons among the brokers' offices. He has
been a sort of fly-about these last years,
into this, that, and every little pitiful
scheme, to turn a dollar, and having a
desk always in the office of the latest
man he could interest in his projects ,
so he is about as hard to find as the
proverbial needle in the hay-mow.

Nobody is specially interested in
keeping track of him, now that he is
down.

Well, in my hunt, I ran upon a Mr.
Filmore who told me where he boards
—a cheap and shabby place, poor fel-

low. He was not there; has n't been
for two weeks or more. Landlady sur-
mised he had gone to join his family
somewhere out West—in California, she
guessed—did n't know when he would
be back; did n't know that he would

ever be back. Oh, yes, she supposed
he *would* be back *some time*,—no, he
had n't left any address to have his
mail forwarded. The purveyor of hash
supposed Mr. Parsons received his mail

at his office—he certainly did not receive any there. Was I a detective? Had Mr. Parsons been getting into trouble? Oh, Cy, the misery of being very poor after having been very rich! The Lord deliver me from it! Poor Parsons, one of the finest and proudest of gentlemen, to be spoken of in such a tenor at the street door of a cheap boarding-house!

Is it any wonder his brave, good little girl is frantic to do something to help him onto his feet again and out of such an atmosphere?

He may be in Colorado; and if he is, you may be called upon to record the sudden death of that scamp Ketchum, any day.

I returned to Mr. Filmore's office to leave a note with him for Parsons, and he told me all about K. The fellow is a thorough scamp and all

his faults are aggravated by his smooth
and oily hypocrisy. It is true he has a
family here, as I mentioned yesterday,
and that he maintains them in a show
of comfort and respectability; but his
wife is a broken-hearted, dispirited creature, whom he married at the muzzle
of a frantic father's gun. He drags her
to church to keep up appearances; but
that is all the respect or civility he
shows her. When he was rich here, he
kept a blonde angel of the demi-monde
in swell style, with her carriage and all that, while his
wife was left to stump
around on foot, with an oc-
casional excursion in company with the hired girl and
the baby on the street-cars
of a Sunday afternoon. Filmore says
the wretch has ruined four or five
poor girls in succession, who came to

work in his office, and started them out
on a sea of sin.

I hope Parsons has gone to Colorado,
so that he may know just where his
daughter is.   I intended to give him
my opinion of the matter very plainly,
if I had found him.

You must keep a kindly eye on the
poor child, Cy, and help her if you
can. Roast that scoundrel and show up
his rotten record and his swindling
scheme, if he gives you half a chance
to open on him.   Jump him any way,
and don't wait for a special provoca-
tion.

Filmore's address—Stanley R. Filmore
—is room 199 Marine Building, Chicago, and he will willingly supply you
with facts enough from the man's ne-
farious record to drive him out of Colorado with his swindling mining
schemes.   It ought to be done—of

course only if the mine is a fake—for that sort of scamps and swindlers are the ones who are bringing mining propositions into disrepute in the East and making it almost impossible to raise money for legitimate enterprises. But I must close. Can you read this wild scrawl?
                                Yours,
                                        Fitz-Mac.

VII.

Creede, Colo., April 13, '93.

Dear Fitz :—Your letter of the 9th, in which you hasten to undo what you did for Ketchum in the preceding letter, if it had no other purpose, was unnecessary. You can never make me believe that a man who eats mashed potatoes with a knife, dips his soup toward him and lets his trousers trail in the mud, has been brought up in respectable society. If anything more was needed to convince me that Ketchum was a shark, it was supplied by him when he told Wygant that he regarded "advertising as unprofessional and unnecessary." The newspapers, he said, did more harm than good. Now, when you hear a man talk that way, you can gamble that he is working the shells and that his game won't stand airing.

In speaking of the embarrassment of becoming very poor after having been very rich, you amuse me, by praying to be delivered from that awful condition. Rest easy, my good fellow. If you follow your chosen path, that of mixing literature with mining, you will doubtless be independently poor the balance of your days.

Well, Miss Parsons is here. She is boarding at the Albany. The Albany is all right. It is the best place in the gulch ; but, of course, you never know who is going to occupy the next seat. Last night, at dinner, the Rev. Tom Uzzell, the city editor and Soapy sat at one table ; a murderer, a gambler, a hand-painted skirt-dancer and a Catholic priest held ˙ another, while Miss Parsons, Billy Woods, the prize-fighter, English Harry and I, ate wild duck at a large table near the stove. I introduced Harry, who is an estimable young man, belonging to one of the best families in Denver, with the hope that Miss Parsons might have an opportunity to see the difference between a real gentleman and that social leper, Ketchum. After dinner I told Harry that I wanted him to make love to Miss Parsons.

" But, I don't love her," says he.

" No matter," says I.

" It's wicked," says he.

"It's right," says I. "It will save her from a life of misery."

"What's the matter with you?" says he. "If it's the proper thing to make love to a sweet young woman whom you don't love, why don't you do it?"

I told him that I was too busy—that I had n't any love that I was not using—that I had done my share in that line. Still he was serious; but finally promised to be a near relative, if he could not love her.

I think I shall open an agency for the protection of unprotected girls. I had luncheon at Upper Creede yesterday, and was shocked when Inez Boyd came in with fresh drug-store hair. Fitz, she is not so beautiful as Miss Parsons; but she is in greater danger, because she is not so strong, and has not had the advantage of early training as Miss Parsons has.

"Jimmie," said I to the little devil this morning, "I want you to take a bundle of papers; go up the gulch until you come to the office of the Sure Thing Mining Company; go in and try to sell a paper. You may take an hour each day for this and loaf as long as you care to in the office, unless they kick you out."

"Sure thing they'll do that," said Jimmie.

"Stop! Keep an eye on Mr. Ketchum, and tell me how many people are working in the office."

Two hours later Jimmie came in with his pockets filled with silver. "Sold all my papers," said he, as he fell over the coal scuttle. "Ketchum bought 'em all to get rid of me. Guess he wanted to talk to that girl he had in the office. Say, she's a bute. Must got 'er in Denver; they don't grow like that in dis gulch. They was a scrappin' like married people when I went in, and he wanted to throw me out. Not on your life, I told him; I'm the devil on the *Chronicle* and dat gang'll burn you up if ye monkey wid me."

"What were they quarreling about, Jimmie?"

"O, 'bout where she was to room, an' he told her she could sleep in de private office; an' you ort to see her then! Mama! but she did lock up his forms for him in short order. Then she said she'd go home; but she'd like to see the mine 'fore she worked fur stock. She's no chump. Say, he aint got no mine."

"You think not, Jimmie?" I said to encourage him.

"Naw. I went over to the Candle office and Lute Johnson's goin' to cremate 'em nex' issue."

I learned to-day that Ketchum had been accepting money from tenderfeet, promising to issue stock, as soon as the stock-books can be printed. I learn also that the Sure Thing Mining Company has no legal existence; that the Sure Thing claim belongs to Ketchum personally.

The camp continues to produce sorrow and silver at the regular ratio of sixteen to one. Old Hank Phelan, of St. Joe, died on the sidewalk in front of the Orleans Club last night. I showed my ignorance by asking a gang who stood round the dead man, at the coroner's inquest, who the distinguished dead might be.

"Say, pardner," said one of the sporty boys, "I reckon you don't ever look in a paper. Don't know Hank Phelan, as licked big Ed. Brown, terror of Oklahoma?" And they all went inside and left me to grope my way out of the dense ignorance that had settled about me.

Bob Ford and Joe Palmer, with a pair of forty - five's, closed all the business houses and put the camp to bed at 9 : 30, one night last week. In an excited effort to escape, the New York *Sun* man and the city editor broke into the dormitory of the Hotel Beebee, where the help slept, and two of the table girls who had been protecting against them, jumped out of a window into the river.

A man was killed by a woman in Upper Creede the other night.

The City Marshal, Captain Light, concluded that Red McCann was a menace to good government and so removed him. His funeral, which occurred last Sunday, was well attended. There was some talk next day by McCann's friends. They even went so far as to hold an inquest; but Cap was well connected, being a brother-in-law to Sapolio, and he was spirited away.

The *Chronicle* is not on a paying basis yet. The twelve hundred dollars has disappeared ; and I have transferred my personal savings here to pay the printers. The schedule is the same and I am working for ·nothing. We have had a strike. Yesterday was a pay day and Freckled Jimmie, the devil, went out at 6 p. m. Jimmie had been with us through all these days of doubt and danger, and when he failed to show up this morning, I confess to a feeling of loneliness. Another boy dropped in to take Jimmie's place; but he was not freckled and I doubted him. About 10 the new boy went to the post-office. He never came back. I remarked that it was not becoming in the editor of a great daily to sit and pine for a boy; and yet, I could not shake off that feeling of neglect that came to me in the early morning and stayed all day. We expected the devil to call upon us, looking to a compromise; but he failed to call. Along in the P. M.-ness, we sent a committee to wait upon Jimmie and ask him to visit the office. He came in, chewing a willow bough.

"Well, Jimmie," I began, "How would it suit you to come back to work at a raise of a dollar a week?"

"Well," said the striker, "I don't kere ef I do or not; but ef you'll let it lap back, over last week, I'll go you. But mind, you don't call me 'Freck' no more. My name's Jimmie from now on, see?" Jimmie is working.

Hope I may be able to give you some good news in my next. So-long,

Cy Warman.

VIII.

TELEGRAM.

New York, April 13, 1892.

The young person's paternal is here and in great luck again. He will wire funds to-day in your care, to make sure of not falling into wrong hands. Deliver message to person yourself, to avoid mistake. Look sharp. Letter by first mail explains all. Address Hoffman House. Fitz-Mac.

IX.

Hoffman House,
　　New York, April 13.

Dear Warman :—The most surprising thing in life is the number of surprises one encounters. Whom should I meet at breakfast here this morning, but Tom Parsons—no longer the broken and rejected man I have pictured to you, but flushed with s u c c e s s and swimming on top of Hope's effulgent tide.

Some New York brokers who had known him in better days and who had confidence in his sagacity and nerve desiring to inaugurate a big grain deal in Chicago, sent for him to come and steer the game. He was as cool to their propositions as if he had had a million

to put in, and demanded a good percentage of the profits. They agreed to
his terms. He has stood behind the
curtain here for three weeks, and in the
name of a dealer here not supposed to
be strong, has engineered the corner
and led the Chicago fellows into the
net. There was a great deal of money
up, and the weak firm which the Chicago operators expected to cinch proved
to be only a stool-pigeon, for a very
strong syndicate.

They settled yesterday, and Tom's
share of the profits is a little over a
hundred thousand. What a freak of
fortune! Though outwardly perfectly
cool, I could see that Parsons is deeply
affected by this turn of the tide, which
puts him on his feet again. It is nothing but gambling after all, and his
mind is flushed and warped by the sudden success. He is full of great proj-

ects to capture millions again. No
doubt the success of this deal gives him
a big pull here, and he is such a bold
and experienced operator that no one
can say what may not happen. But
this insatiate passion for high and reckless play has injured him, mentally and
morally. He confessed to me after we
went to his room, that he had not once
thought of his family during the three
weeks he has been here,—that is, not of
their condition and their needs. Think
of that, in the most tender of husbands,

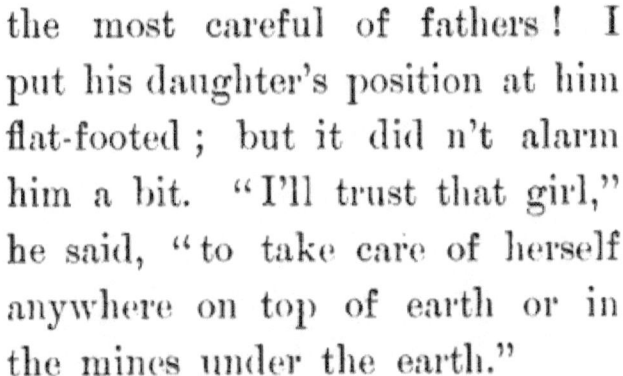

the most careful of fathers! I
put his daughter's position at him
flat-footed ; but it did n't alarm
him a bit. "I'll trust that girl,"
he said, "to take care of herself
anywhere on top of earth or in
the mines under the earth."

"Would you trust her to work, live
and lodge in the slums of Chicago or

down here about Five Points in New
York ? " Would you want to expose
her to such an existence ? Especially if
she was likely to encounter in these
places a few refined men of reckless
habits, who would be sure to misunder-
stand her position and whose very
sympathy would be her greatest danger ? Well, that's what Creede is,
Tom," said I, " if you just add the
physical exposure of a mountain cli-
mate in a camp where the best house
is no better than a shanty built of wet,
unseasoned lumber."

He promised me he would telegraph
money to her to-day and advise her to
go to her mother. He laughed at my
fears about Ketchum's designs, and said
he would trust his girl against a dozen
Ketchums ; but he was not insensible
to the danger that the scamp might
bring scandal on her, and I worked

him on that line till he promised to
go right away and telegraph money to
her. I gave him your address and he
will send in your care, to prevent the
possibility of his message falling into
K's hands. That is why I have just
wired you. I can realize that, even in
Creede, it will compromise the girl to
have any connection with that Sure
Thing outfit, and expose her character
to suspicion. Before this reaches you,
no doubt, she will have gone home,
and I shall have no further occasion
to write you about her; but still, if
you have an idle hour, you may write
me here and tell me how Ketchum is
working his game. While I have no
further anxiety about Miss P., I confess to a curiosity to know if the anxiety I did have was well grounded.

How are you getting on with the
paper? Every one wants to hear about

Creede here, and I believe you could get up a big subscription list in Wall street if you had a canvasser in the field. Everybody has the most exaggerated notions of the extent and richness of the camp, and the newspaper people are as wild as the rest. They have the most childish notions—I mean the common run of men only, of course—as to the condition of silver mining. Their idea of a bonanza is a place where pure silver is quarried out like building stone. You could n't possibly tell them any fake story of the richness of mines they would n't believe. In fact, you can make them believe anything else easier than the truth. This fact hurts our business dreadfully, too, in the East and creates a prejudice against the use

of silver as money. It also helps the
mining sharps who are working frauds.
I shall have a curiosity to see how you
roast that snide scheme of Ketchum &
Co. Don't fail to send me the paper.

You may address me here for two
weeks.   Affectionately yours,

FITZ-MAC.

X.

CREEDE, COLO., April 20, '92.

DEAR FITZ :—Yes, the surprises in
this life are surprising. We opened a
couple of surprise packages here last
night.   •

I was surprised the other day when
Miss P. came into the office and asked
my advice. Until lately she has en-
deavored to avoid me.

I think Harry has been watering my
stock with the lady, and I am pleased
to note that these young people occupy

a table at the Albany that seats two. Last Sunday, I drifted into the tent where they hold sacred services; it is called the Tabernacle. Miss Parsons was performing on a little cottage organ, while Harry stood near her and sang, " There's a Land that is Fairer than Day."

Ah, yes, in the sweet by-and-by! Is there anything that holds so much for the trusting soul? In the sun-kissed over-yonder, there is rest for the weary. Always full and running over, there is no false bottom in the sweet by-and-by.

Hope springs eternal
In the human breast,
Faith to push the button—
God will do the rest.

I have begun to hope that Harry will love Miss Parsons. What he has done for her already has had a good effect. His society is better for her, just as the sunshine is better for the flowers than the atmosphere of a damp, dark cellar, where lizards creep o'er the sweating stones.

Plenty of fellows here would love her, but for their own amusement. Not so with Harry. He is as serious as though he were in reality an Englishman. Yesterday the young lady was very much worried over a note she had received, and she showed it to me. It ended thus :

> Go, leave me in my misery,
>   And when thou art alone,
> God grant that thou may'st pine for me,
>   As I for thee have pone.

It was signed " Harry," and that's what hurt her heart. I told her it was

Tabor's writing; that his first name was Harry, and she was glad.

As I write this, I look across the street to the barber-shop where Inez Boyd is having her hair cut short. Ye Gods! faded and then amputated! So will be her pure young life. Already the frost of sin has settled around her soul. Youth's bloom has been blighted; her cheeks are hollow; her eyes have a vacant, far-away look. Her mind, mayhap, goes back to her happy home in Denver, where she used to kneel at night and say, "Now I lay me."

She has left her place at the restaurant, and with her partner, that "break away" creature with the yellow hair, is living in a cottage, taking their meals at the Albany.

I must tell you now what Miss Parsons wanted advice about. She had very little to do in the office, and if she would act as cashier in the restaurant at meal time, two hours morning, noon and night, Mr. Sears would allow her ten dollars a week, and her board, or twenty dollars a week, in all. From 9 to 11, and 2 to 4, she could attend to Mr. Ketchum's correspondence. There was still another job open. They wanted an operator across the street at the Western Union from 8 P. M. until 12, when the regular night man came on to take the *Chronicle* press report. If she could take that, it would make her cash income twenty dollars above her board.

I asked her what she intended to do from midnight till morning. She smiled, good-naturedly, and said she thought she would have to sleep some, otherwise she would have asked for a job, folding papers.

I told her that it was all very proper if she could stand the long hours. She said she could always get an hour's sleep after her midday meal, and in that way she would be able to hold it down for a while. I ventured to ask why she failed to reckon her "Sure Thing" salary when counting her cash income. "Oh," she had forgotten. "Mr. Ketchum told her she would have to take her pay in stock." I did not tell her how worthless that stock was, but I determined to have Mr. Ketchum attended to.

Yesterday a quiet caucus was held in the rear of Banigan's saloon, at which a committee of seven was appointed to wait upon Mr. Ketchum and inquire into the affairs of the Sure Thing Mining and Milling Com-

pany, the statement having been made
in the morning *Chronicle* that the company had no legal existence.

Here come the surprises.   In accord-
ance with the arrangements made by
the caucus at Banigan's, the committee
called last night at the office of the
Sure Thing Mining Company and asked

for Mr. Ketchum.   That gentleman
showed how little he knew of camp
life, by ordering them from the room.
The spokesman told him to sit down
and be quiet.   He would not be com-

manded to sit down in his own house, he said, as he jumped upon a table and began to orate on the freedom of America. At that moment one of the party, who is called "Mex" because he came from New Mexico, shied a rope across the room. It hovered around near the canvas ceiling for a second, then settled around the neck of the orator. "Come off the perch," said Mex, as he gave the rope a pull and yanked the speculator from the table.

That did the business. After that the operator only begged that his life be spared.

"Now sir," said the leader, "you will oblige us by answering every question put to you. If you tell the truth you may come out all right, if you lie you will be taking chances."

"We are the executive committee of the Gamblers' Protective Association and we are here to investigate your game. We recognize the right of the dealer to a liberal percentage, but we are opposed to sure thing men and sandbaggers."

" Is the Sure Thing Mining Company incorporated under the laws of Colorado ? "

" Well—it's—un— "

"Stop sir," said the leader. " These questions will be put to you so that you can answer yes or no. I will say further that the committee will know when you tell the truth, so there's a 'hunch for you an' you better play it, see ?"

" Is the Sure Thing Mining Company incorporated ? "

" No."

" Is it true that you have taken money on account of stock to be issued ? "

" Well,—I have."

" Stop ! "

" Yes sir, it is true."

" Have you paid your stenographer ? "

" Yes sir."

" What in ? "

" Stock."

" How many claims do you own and what are they called, where located ? "

" One—Sure Thing. Bachelor Mountain."

" Shipped any ore ? "

" No."

" Any in sight ? "

" No."

" Ever have any assay ? "

" No."

" That'll do."

" Gentlemen," said the leader, " You have heard the questions and answers, all in favor of hangin' this fellow say ' aye.' "

" Contrary ' no.' "

Three to three ; the vote is a tie. I will vote with the ' noes ' we will not hang him.

"All in favor of turning him loose at the lower end of the Bad Lands say ' aye.' "

" Carried, unanimously."

" Mr. Ketchum, I congratulate you."

All this took place in Upper Creede, and about the time the committee were escorting Ketchum down through the gulch, Kadish Bula, the superintendent of the Bachelor, rushed into the Western Union office and handed a dispatch to Miss Parsons, asking her to rush it.

After sending the message, Miss Parsons came to my office where Harry and I were enjoying a quiet chat, in which the two young women in whom I have become so interested, played an important part.

"I beg your pardon," she said with a pretty blush when she opened the door. "I thought you were alone."

Harry was about to leave when she asked him to remain.

With a graceful little jump she landed on the desk in front of me, and

looking me straight in the face she said:

"I want to ask you a few questions

and I want you to answer me truthfully."

"Is the Sure Thing Mining Company any good ?"

"No," said I, and she never flinched.

"Is Ketchum's location of the Sure Thing claim a valid one ?"

"That I cannot answer, for I don't know," said I.

"Do you think Mr. Bula of the Bachelor would know ?" was her next question.

We both agreed that he ought to be excellent authority on locations in general, and especially good in this case, as theirs was an adjoining property."

"How, and when, can a claim be relocated ?" she asked with a steady look in my face.

I asked her to wait a moment, and I called Mr. Vaughan. I go to him for everything that I fail to find in the dictionary.

In a very few moments the expert explained to the young lady that a claim located in '90 upon which no assessment work was done in '91, was open for relocation in '92.

That was exactly what she wanted to know, she said, as she shot out of the door and across the street to the telegraph office.

Before we had time to ask each other what she meant, a half dozen citizens walked through the open door.

"We have just returned from Wason, where we went with Ketchum," said the leader.

"His game is dead crooked, and we told him to duck, and we want to ask about his typewriter, an' see 'f she's got any dough."

I explained that Miss Parsons was across the street, working in the telegraph office.

"Miss Parsons," said the leader as he entered the office, "we have just escorted your employer out of camp, and I reckon we put you out of a job; we want to square ourselves with you."

"Oh, I'm all right," she said, glad to know that they had n't hanged the poor devil. "I am working half time at the restaurant and until midnight here."

Without saying a word, the leader held out his hand to one of the men who dropped a yellow coin into it, another did the same, and before she knew what it meant, the spokesman stacked seven tens upon her table, said good-night, and they left the room.

"Will you work for me for an hour or so," said the girl as the night man entered the office. Of course he would, but he was disappointed. His life in the camp had been a lonely one till this beautiful woman came to work in the office. He had dropped in two hours ahead of time just to live in the sunshine of her presence.

"There's a tip for you," she said as she flipped the top ten from the stack of yellows in front of the operator, dropped the other six into her hand-bag and jumped out into the night.

"Here I am again," she laughed as she opened my door. "I want you to put that in your safe till morning;" and she planked sixty dollars in gold, down on my desk.

"Bless you, Miss Parsons," said I, "we don't keep such a thing. We always owe the other fellow, but I'll give it to Vaughan, he does n't drink."

"I want you and Harry to go with me," she said, "and ask no questions. Put on your overcoats, there are three good horses waiting at the door."

In thirty minutes from that time, our horses were toiling up the Last Chance trail, and in an hour, we stood on the summit of Bachelor, eleven thousand feet above the sea.

The scene was wondrously beautiful. Below, adown the steep mountain-side, lay the long, dark trail leading to the gulch where the arc lights gleamed on the trachyte cliffs. Around a bend in the valley, came a silvery stream—the broad and beautiful Rio Grande, its crystal ripples gleaming in the soft light

of a midnight moon. Away to the east,
above, beyond the smaller mountains,
the marble crest of the Sangre de
Christo stood up above the world.

Turning from this wondrous picture I
saw the horses with their riders just

entering a narrow trail that lay through an aspen grove in the direction of the Bachelor mine. Harry had secured a board from the Bachelor shaft-house and was driving a stake on the Sure Thing claim when I arrived.

"So this is what you are up to Miss Parsons," said I, taking in the situation at a glance."

"Yes, sir," she said, "I have written my name on that stake and I propose to put men to work to-morrow."

It was just midnight when we reached the telegraph office, and Miss Parsons showed us the telegram which Mr. Bula had sent : it read :

"*John Herrick,*

Denver Club, Denver :

Got Amethyst vein. Sure Thing can be bought for one thousand, or can re-locate and fight them ; belongs to Ketchum. Answer."

" Well," said Harry, "you're all right."

"Now," said Miss Parsons, "I want to find Mr. Ketchum and give him a check for one thousand and get a bill of sale or something to show."

We explained that Ketchum was at that time walking in the direction of Wagon Wheel Gap. Further, that unless she had that amount of money in the bank, she would be doing a serious thing to give a check.

"Ah, but I have," she said with a smile," as she pulled a bank-book from her desk. "My father wired a thousand dollars to the Miners' and Merchants' Bank for me a few days ago ; the telegram notifying me it was there, came in your care, and I must apologize for not having told you sooner, but I was afraid you might ask me to give up my place, if you learned how rich I was."

"You are all right, Miss Parsons," said I, "and I congratulate you—but there is no excuse for you wanting to give that scamp a thousand dollars."

"Then I must ask another favor of you," she said. "I want ten men to go to work on the Sure Thing to-morrow."

At my request, Harry promised to have the men at work by nine o'clock, and as I write this I can hear the blasts and see the white smoke puffiing from the Sure Thing claim. Just now I see Harry and the "Silver Queen" coming down the trail. They are riding this way; Harry is holding a piece of rock in his left hand; they are talking about it, and they both look very happy. Aye, verily, the surprises are surprising; hope springs eternal.

Good-by,

CY WARMAN.

XI.

HOFFMAN HOUSE,
NEW YORK, April 27, '92.

MY DEAR CY:—Your last letter is a daisy. I read it with all the interest of a novel.

What a magic camp Creede must be, after all! It was manly in those vigilantes who hustled Ketchum out of camp so unceremoniously to treat our little friend, Polly, so generously and so delicately— but it is characteristic of the West.

She is a courageous and capable girl, isn't she?—her quickness of wit in jumping that Sure Thing claim shows it.

I'm glad you like her, and I knew you would, if you got to know the quick and courageous spirit that is in her. She did n't waste a day crying over spilt milk when her pap busted and all the ease and luxuries and adulations that surround a rich man's daughter vanished from about her like dew before the sun, but just jumped in and went to learning how to earn her own living and help take care of the family.

Would n't it be romantic, though, if that mine should really prove a bonanza!—I declare I get excited thinking about it. I suppose there is actually a chance that it may, since it is on the same vein—or is supposed to be—as the Amethyst mine. Would n't that be too good! How lucky that she happened to be in the telegraph office when that dispatch was sent! And oh, say, you and Harry, ain't you the dandy span to have such a pretty girl as Polly in your care—and put there by yours confidingly, don't forget. No, don't you *dare* forget, for you would never have known Polly but for me, and Harry would n't have got acquainted with her probably, but for you. It is lucky I happened to know your heart was already anchored, or I should never have introduced you.

So Harry refused to fall in love with her, did he, when you issued your orders? Well, I'll bet you a horse and buggy he will fall in love with her before he is a month older, unless he is in love with some other girl, for Polly is one of the most interesting girls I have ever seen.

I don't know Harry very well, but my impressions are, he is an unusually nice fellow. If he is only half as manly and smart as he looks, I shall put in the good word for him with Polly.

I can see from what you write, she likes him already—and likes you also, or she would never treat you both with such confidence. But she will lead Harry a dance before ever he captures her—you bet she will—for she has a touch of the coquette in her nature in spite, also, of the warmest and most loyal of hearts.

I hope he *will* fall in love with her; it will do him good, even if nothing comes of it. A fellow whose nature is not morbid, is never any the worse off for loving a good little girl like Polly, even if she do not recipro-cate. It may cost him some pain, but he will live it through, and no man's nature ever expands to its full capacity till the fever of an honest passion gets

into his blood—but you know how that
is yourself, Cy.

I knew about her jumping the mine
before your letter came—the bare fact
only—for I have met Parsons here
every day and he showed me a cipher
dispatch from her telling him. It seems
she knew his old cipher and used it.
He translated it to me in the greatest
admiration of her pluck and quickness.
Probably she never would have done it
if she had n't had you two fellows to
stand by her. Bully boys! I know
you are behaving all right, or she
would n't trust you.

You may tell Harry all I have told
you about the dreadful straits in which
her family have been, so that he will
perfectly understand how she came to
go down to Creede. I would n't have
him think cheaply of her for anything,
for I have got it all fixed in my mind

that he is to fall head over heels in love with her. I do not believe she has had a serious thought of any other fellow, for, though as a young Miss she was quite a favorite in Chicago, it is not likely she formed any serious attachments—any attachment that would stand the strain of poverty such as the Parsons have gone through in the last three years. Since she and her mother have been in Denver, I know they have refused to make acquaintances and have kept proudly to themselves. So I venture to guess the field is clear for Harry if he is lucky enough to interest her, and you are fairly safe in speaking the encouraging word to him. As I have said, it will do him good to get the fever in his blood, even if he should fail.

Like her father, Polly is very swift and decisive in her judgments of peo-

ple, and very self-reliant. The girl has
always been in love with her father, and
Tom has always treated her more like a
lover than a father. He is awfully
proud of her, and he brags about her
to me every time we meet. But he is
anxious, nevertheless, about her being
in that camp, and he is leaving to-
night to join her, and I fancy he will
bring her away. You may know how
anxious he feels in spite of all his brag
about her pluck and smartness and her
ability to take care of herself, when he
abandons the irons he has in the fire
here, to go out and look after her. He
admires the business spirit in her and
upholds it, but still he is afraid that
fighting her own way in such a rough
place will make her coarse and un-
lovely.

Tell Harry to put his best foot for-
ward and make his best impression on

the old man, if you find him caring
seriously for Polly, for she is likely to
go a good deal according to her father's
fancy in the matter of a sweetheart. If
he gets the old man's heart, the battle
for Polly is more than half won—that
is, if she already likes him a little bit,
which I am pretty sure from what you
write she does. Of course, you will
manage to let the old man know what
a respectful admiration both you and
Harry have had for Polly, and how,
being very busy, *you* have rather left it
to your friend, Mr. English, a young
gentleman of good judgment and re-
sponsible character and all that, to
keep an eye on her interests and make
himself serviceable in case she needed
counsel, etc., etc.

But above all, make him think—both
you and Harry—that his girl has n't
really needed the protection of either of

you, but has pa ed her own canoe
like a veteran. That will please him
more than anything else, and it would
irritate his pride a little to think you
had been necessary to her.

You will get this probably before he
arrives, for he will stop half a day in
Denver to see his wife and boy; so be
on your good behavior, both of you,
and don't shock him.

What you tell me about that poor
girl from Denver—Inez, is that her
name?—is distressing. Her first bleach-
ing her hair and then cutting it off,
shows plainly enough the course her
young footsteps are taking. That
sharp-faced, wiry little blonde she
chums with has no doubt led her into
evil ways. There is no company so
dangerous for a girl as a bad woman.
Could n't you take her aside and give
her a talking to, and advise her to go

home to her family ? Take her up to one of the dance-halls some night, and show her the beer-soaked, painted hags that haunt these places to pick up the means of a wretched and precarious existence, and let her know that is where she will bring up, if she keeps on. But I suppose she is past talking to— past turning back.

Write me the latest news about Polly's mine and how it is turning out, and how Harry and Polly are making it. I am deeply interested.

Yours,

FITZ-MAC.

XII.

CREEDE, Colo., May 9, 1892.

DEAR FITZ :—I have to tell you a sad story now.

Last Saturday I went to Denver, and as I entered the train at this place, I

noticed some men bringing an invalid
into the car. One of the men asked
the porter to look after the sick girl
in "lower two," and I gathered from
that that she was alone. I had section
three, and as soon as the train pulled
out I noticed that the sick person grew
restless. We had been out less than
thirty minutes when she began to roll
and toss about, and talk as people do
when sick with mountain fever.

When the Durango car, which was a
buffet, was switched to our train at
Alamosa, I went to the sick berth and
asked the sufferer if she would like a
cup of tea and some toast. She was
very ill, but she seemed glad to have
some one talk to her, and as she answered "yes," almost in a whisper, she
turned . her poor, tired, tearful eyes to
me, and with a little show of excite-
ment that started her coughing, spoke

my name. It was Inez Boyd. I should
not have known her, but I had seen her
after she had bleached her beautiful
hair, and later when she was in the
barber-shop.   As the gold of sunset,
that marked the end of a beautiful
spring day, shone in through the car

window, it fell upon her
pale face, where a faint
flush on her thin cheeks
spoke of the fever within,
and showed that the end of
a life was near.

She took a swallow or two of the
tea, looked at the toast and pushed it
away. She had been ill for a week,
she said, and had eaten nothing for
two days. I did what little I could
for her comfort, and when I went to
say good-night, she held my hand ; the
tears, one after another, came from the

deep, dark eyes, fell across the pale
cheeks, and were lost in the ghastly
yellow hair.

"Don't think I weep because I am
afraid of death," she said. "I am so
glad now, that I know that it's all
over, but I am sorry for mamma ; it will
kill her."

I asked, and she gave me her address in Denver, and I promised to
call. .

When the train stopped at the gate
of the beautiful city, she had called
her home, some men came with an invalid chair, and when I saw them take
her to a carriage I hurried on to my
hotel.

That afternoon I called to ask after
the girl. The windows were open, and
I could see a few people standing
about the room with bowed heads.
Dr. O'Connor came down the little

walk that lay from the door of a neat cottage to the street, and without recognizing me, closed the gate softly, turned his back to me and hurried away.

Inez Boyd was dead. God in His mercy, had called her away to save her from a life of sorrow, sin and shame, and He called her just in time.

In the "Two Voices," Tennyson says :

"Whatever crazy sorrow saith,
  No life that breathes with human breath
  Has ever truly longed for death."

I don't believe it. There are times in life—in some lives, at least—when nothing is more desirable than death.

XIII.

CREEDE, COLO., May 13, 1892.

MY DEAR FITZ :—You ask me how the *Chronicle* is doing. It is doing better than the editor. I have been reducing expenses on every hand, but since the state land sale, the boom has collapsed, so that from one hundred dollars a week, we have got up to where we lose three hundred a week, with a good prospect for an increase. The responsibility has grown so great, that I begin to feel like a Kansas farm, struggling to bear up under a second mortgage.

I have been elected assistant superintendent of the Sunday-school, umpired a prize-fight, been time-keeper at a ball game, have been elected to the common council from the Bad Lands by an overwhelming vote, but I have received no salary as editor of the *Chronicle.*

Tabor has written another note, and perpetrated some more poetry :

" Among these rose-bejeweled hills
    Where bloom the fairest flowers

Where the echo from the mines and mills
This little vale with music fills,
   We spent life's gladdest hours.

"And still within this limpid stream
   Where sports the speckled trout,
Her mirrored-face doth glow and gleam;
'Twas here I grappled love's young dream—
   And here my light went out."

Is n't that enough to drive a young woman to cigarettes? Some girls it might, but it will never disturb Polly Parsons.

If I did not know Harry as I do, I should say he was learning to love Miss Parsons very rapidly, now that she is rich, but I will not do him that injustice. He has loved her all along, but the prospect of losing her is what makes him restless now. Men who have lived as long as you and I have, know how hard it is to ride by

the side of a beautiful woman over
these grand mountains on a May morning, without making love to her;

When the restless hand of Nature
  Reaches out to shift the scene,
And the brooks begin to warble in the dell;
When the waking fields are fluffy
  And the meadow-lands are green,
And the tassels on the trees begin to swell.

Ah, these are times that try men's
hearts; but poor Harry, he is so timid;
why I should have called her down a
month ago, if I had his hand.

She is too honest to encourage him
if she does n't really care for him, but
she must, she can't help it, he is almost
an ideal young man. Maybe that is
where he falls down; I've heard it
said that a man who is *too* nice, is
never popular with the ladies. Perhaps that is why you and I are pour-

ing our own coffee to-day. Swinburne says—

"There is a bitterness in things too sweet."

Polly's father is here. He brought a Chicago capitalist with him, and the Sure Thing has been sold for sixty-one thousand dollars. I was sorry to learn of the sale, for it will take away from the camp one of the richest and rarest flowers that has ever adorned these hills.

Since the great fire, we have all moved to the Tortoni, on the border of the Bad Lands. The parlor is very small, and last night when Harry and the "Silver Queen," as we call her now, were talking while I pretended to be reading a newspaper, I could not help hearing some of the things they said. Harry wanted her photograph, but she would not give it. She said

she never gave her pictures to young
men, under any circumstances. When
she found a young man with whom
she could trust her photo, she said she
would give him the original. Harry
said something very softly then; I did

not hear what it was, but she said
very plainly, very seriously, that she
would let him know before she left.

"And you go to-morrow?" he asked,

and it seemed to me that there were tears in his voice.

"Yes," she said, with a sigh that hinted that she was not altogether glad to go. "Papa has bought the old place back again; we shall stop in Denver for mamma and my little brother, and then return to the dear old home where I have spent so many happy days—where I learned to lisp the prayers that I have never forgotten to say in this wicked camp; and I feel now that God has heard and answered me. It may seem almost wicked, but I am half sorry to leave this place; you have all been so kind to me; but it is best. Father will give you our address, and now, how soon may we expect you in Chicago?"

"How soon may I come?—next week —next year?"

"Not next year," she said quickly;

and although I was looking at my paper, I saw him raise her hand to his lips.

"And will you give me your photo then ?" he asked.

"Yes," she whispered, and I wanted to jump and yell, but I was afraid she might change her mind.

"I wish you would sing one song for me before you go," said Harry, after they had been silent for some moments.

"What shall it be ?"

"When other lips," he answered.

"But there should be no other lips," said the bright and charming woman.

"I know there should not, and I hope there may not, but sing it anyway and I will try to be strong and unafraid."

As Miss Parsons went to the piano, I left the room, left them alone, and as I went out into the twilight, I

heard the gentle notes as the light
fingers wandered over the keys.

"When other lips and other hearts—"
  Came drifting through the trees.
"In language whose excess imparts,"
  Was borne upon the breeze.
  Ah, hope is sweet and love is strong
    And life's a summer sea;
  A woman's soul is in her song;
  "And you'll remember me."

Still rippling from her throbbing throat
  With joy akin to pain,
There seemed a tear in every note,
  A sob in every strain.
Soft as the twilight shadows creep
  Across the listless lea,
The singer sang her love to sleep
  With, "You'll remember me."

Truly yours,
CY WARMAN.